A Glorious Year

A Glorious Year

Dr. Sarah ShaBazz

CONTENTS

For the teachers who loved us on purpose and taught us our worth before the world tried to define it.

SEP
SHABAZZ ENTERPRISE
PUBLISHING

1. Glorious Baptist Day School

Glorious Baptist Day School was more than a building. It was a community anchor tucked quietly into the rhythm of a residential neighborhood in Los Angeles. Nestled in the middle of the block, it felt almost hidden, surrounded by modest homes that softened the presence of the school. Between the school and the large church that stood proudly on the corner were houses, reminding everyone that education, faith, and family life were deeply connected in that neighborhood.

The school itself was a one-story structure with eight classrooms arranged in an L-shape. From the outside, it had a humble, almost fragile appearance, as if it were being gently held upright by the visible support poles placed between each classroom. Those poles gave the building a distinct look, as if each room stood independently while still connected to the others, much like the children and families it served.

Because it sat in the middle of the block, there was a sense of safety and enclosure. The surrounding homes created a protective atmosphere. Children arrived not to a grand campus, but to a space that felt personal and intimate. You could almost hear the echoes of laughter bouncing off the walls and into the neighborhood streets.

At the opposite corner of the block stood the nursery school. Its location marked the beginning of a child's educational journey, while the day school carried that journey forward. Together, the church on the corner, the nursery school, and Glorious Baptist Day School formed a triangle of spiritual grounding, early learning, and community development.

The physical structure may have been simple, eight rooms, one story, L-shaped, supported by poles, but its impact was anything but small. Schools like that often hold generational memories: first prayers recited, first letters written, friendships formed, and values shaped within walls that may have looked modest but carried great meaning.

Before Everything Changed

I had been at Glorious Baptist Day School since second grade, but most of the students in my class had been there even longer, since kindergarten. Some of us had learned our letters in the same rooms where we now practiced long division. We had grown up together inside those walls.

By fifth grade, the school felt like family.

We knew which classrooms used to be bedrooms and which one had once been the dining room. We knew the creaky floorboard near the reading shelf and how the heater knocked three times before it came on. We lined up the same way every morning and sat in nearly the same seats year after year.

Only two students had joined us back in third grade. Everyone else had been there as long as we could remember.

Until this school year started.

That year felt different from the beginning.

Some students left during the first month and a half of school. Their desks stayed empty for weeks before the principal finally moved the rest of us closer together. Nobody explained why they left. They just disappeared, like chalk wiped clean from the board.

Our teacher was Mrs. Gray.

Mrs. Gray was new to Glorious Baptist Day School that year, along with her entire family. She had five children, and every one of them attended the school. There was a Gray child in almost every classroom: kindergarten, second grade, third grade, fifth grade, and sixth grade.

Her daughter Gina was in my fifth-grade class, and her son Gregory was one of the sixth graders who shared our room. The Gray children were light-skinned African American, with sandy brown hair and green eyes, the kind of eyes that made people stare a little longer than they meant to.

Mrs. Gray was a big woman. She spent most of the day sitting at her desk. She taught us from there, reading lessons, writing assignments, Bible verses, all delivered from behind her chair.

She did not walk around the room.

She did not stand at the chalkboard.

She did not move much at all.

Most days, we read quietly from our workbooks or copied sentences until our fingers cramped. When someone raised a hand, Mrs. Gray would answer without getting up. Her voice carried, but not far enough to reach the back row where the sixth graders sat.

The room felt heavy.

The days felt long.

Sometimes I watched the clock above the door and wondered why time moved slower inside our classroom than anywhere else in the school.

Nobody said anything was wrong.

But everyone could feel it.

Something was not working.

And none of us knew yet that everything was about to change.

Mrs. Gray's Classroom

Mrs. Gray's classroom was not loud.

It was not wild.

It was not even especially disobedient.

It was simply tired.

The desks sat in rows, but not neat ones. The room always looked a little off, as if no one had taken the time to straighten what had drifted out of place. Workbooks stayed stacked. Papers waited. The chalkboard carried half-finished notes from lessons that did not seem fully alive.

Most of the day, Mrs. Gray remained seated at her desk.

She taught from there. She corrected from there. She watched from there.

She rarely moved between the rows. She rarely leaned over a shoulder. She rarely came to the back of the room where the sixth graders sat. The classroom felt divided, not by walls, but by distance.

We did our work.

We copied scripture.

We completed sentences.

We turned pages.

But something in the room felt flat, as though school had become a place where we passed time instead of entered it.

Even as children, we could feel the difference between a room that was being managed and a room that was being led.

Mrs. Gray's classroom was being managed.

Barely.

And then one afternoon, the door opened.

The Afternoon Everything Changed

The afternoon Mrs. Grace arrived started like every other one.
We lined up outside the classroom door after lunch with our hands behind our backs. The sixth graders stood in the rear, pre-

tending not to notice us fifth graders whispering. The bell rang late again. It always rang late when we had substitutes.

Inside, the desks sat quiet and crooked, like they had given up trying to stay straight.

We were halfway through copying the daily scripture when the door opened.

Not slowly.

Not quietly.

It opened with purpose.

A woman stepped inside wearing heels that clicked sharply against the floor, click, click, click, louder than anything we had heard in that room all year.

Every head lifted.

She was short. Very short. Almost the same height as some of the fifth graders. If she had not been wearing heels at least four inches high, she might have been mistaken for a student walking into the wrong classroom.

But there was nothing student-like about her.

Her hair was styled in a way none of us had ever seen before. The front was smooth and neat, pressed close to her head, but the back was something else entirely, a thick cascade of shiny curls clipped into place, bouncing when she moved. The curls curved softly around her neck like a cloud of movement.

Some of us stared, trying to figure out where her real hair ended and the rest began.

She wore real makeup, lipstick that matched her nails. Her dress was pressed and fitted, and her jacket matched her shoes exactly.

She did not look like a teacher.

She looked like someone important.

She stopped in the middle of the room.

"Good afternoon," she said.

Her voice was calm, smooth, and confident.

Nobody answered.

She lifted one eyebrow slightly.

"I said, good afternoon."

"Good afternoon, Mrs...?" someone mumbled.

She turned to the chalkboard and wrote her name in clean, looping cursive.

Mrs. Grace.

She rested one hand lightly on the desk and looked around the room slowly, as if she were memorizing each of our faces.

"My name is Mrs. Grace," she said. "And before we begin, I believe introductions are important."

She did not rush. She did not fidget. She stood as if she had always belonged there.

"I am new to teaching," she continued. "Before coming here, I worked as a nurse."

A few gasps floated across the room.

"A real nurse?" someone whispered.

Mrs. Grace smiled. "Yes. A real nurse. I worked in a hospital for many years."

That changed things.

Nurses were serious. Nurses knew things about life and death and emergencies. Suddenly, we were not just looking at a substitute teacher. We were looking at someone who had chosen to be there.

"I took care of bodies," she said, folding her hands gently. "Now I intend to take care of minds."

The room fell completely silent.

"When I interviewed with Pastor Roberts," she continued, "we discovered something interesting. We are third cousins."

A few students turned around to look at one another.

"Third cousins?" Greg whispered.

"Yes," she said calmly. "We are both from Mississippi. Different towns. Different families. Same roots."

She let that settle for a moment.

"I believe God places us exactly where we are supposed to be."

Then her voice shifted slightly.

"I may be new to teaching," she said, "but I am not new to discipline. And I am not new to expectations."

She placed her purse neatly on the desk and stepped away from the front of the room.

"Hands on desks. Eyes forward."

The room obeyed before anyone realized it had done so.

"I expect respect," she said.

Her heels clicked softly as she walked down the aisle.

"I expect effort."

She paused beside a sixth grader's desk.

"And I expect greatness, from every single one of you."

No teacher had ever used that word about us before.

Greatness.

Not behavior.

Not quiet.

Not compliance.

Greatness.

She walked slowly through every row, leaning over desks, glancing at handwriting, nodding without speaking. When she reached the back of the room, the place no teacher had bothered to go all year, even the sixth graders sat up.

She looked directly at me.

Not through me.

At me.

"We will begin with prayer," she said. "And then we will learn."

After the prayer, she walked the room again, heels clicking softly, curls bouncing behind her.

"This," she said gently, "is going to be a very good year."

I did not know why, but something fluttered in my chest.

For the first time since school started, the classroom felt awake.

And I knew, even before lunchtime, that nothing would ever be the same again.

Mrs. Grace

Mrs. Grace was not the kind of teacher who disappeared behind a desk.

She entered a room and changed it.

Even when she was standing still, she felt in motion. Her heels were planted, her posture straight, her voice measured. She looked at people directly. She expected an answer when she spoke. She expected you to sit up, to pay attention, to try.

She was small, but nothing about her presence was small.

Her curls bounced when she walked. Her nails clicked lightly when she touched the desk. Her clothes were always pressed. Her lipstick was always right. She carried herself with a kind of polished certainty I had never seen in a classroom before.

She did not look like she was simply doing a job.

She looked like she had arrived with purpose.

And maybe that was why we believed her so quickly.

When she said she expected greatness, she did not sound like she was using a nice word to encourage children.

She sounded like she had already decided it was true.

That mattered.

Children can tell the difference between adults who are hoping for something and adults who are expecting it.

Mrs. Grace expected it.

From all of us.

From the fifth graders.

From the sixth graders.

From the talkers.

From the quiet ones.

From the children in the front.

From the children in the back.

She did not lower the room to meet what it had been.

She raised it.

And somehow, almost immediately, we started rising with it.

What I Wasn't Supposed to Hear

Recess was always loud.

The playground behind Glorious Baptist Day School filled with shouting, laughing, and the thumping sound of rubber balls hitting the pavement. Most days I ran outside with everyone else as soon as the bell rang.

But that day I stayed inside.

I was digging through my book satchel looking for the snack my mother had packed for me. Sometimes she wrapped cookies in wax paper, and I hoped that's what I would find.

The classroom was quiet with everyone else outside.

I heard voices.

Mrs. Grace was sitting at her desk talking to one of the girls from our class. I couldn't see them from where I was standing, but I could hear them clearly.

"You didn't write anything on this paper," Mrs. Grace said.

Her voice was calm, but serious.

I peeked up from behind my desk.

Camille was standing beside her.

"You haven't even written your name," Mrs. Grace continued.

There was a long pause.

Then I heard Mrs. Grace say something that surprised me.

"Oh Lord," she whispered softly. "This child can't read."

I froze.

I wasn't supposed to hear that.

Camille just stood there quietly. Her head was down, and she didn't say anything.

Mrs. Grace didn't sound angry. She sounded concerned.

She leaned forward and spoke more gently.

"That's alright," she told Camille. "We're going to work on it."

I quickly looked back down into my book bag so no one would think I had been listening.

A few minutes later the recess bell rang and everyone came running back inside.

No one said anything about what had happened.

And I never told anyone what I had heard.

But from that day forward, something changed.

Every afternoon Mrs. Grace would sit with Camille and practice words. Sometimes it was during reading time. Sometimes it was after school.

Little by little, Camille began to learn.

By the end of fifth grade she could read.

Not perfectly.

But she could read.

Mrs. Grace decided that Camille should repeat fifth grade the following year so she could become stronger before moving on.

Back then I didn't fully understand what I had witnessed.

Now I do.

That was the day I learned that a good teacher does more than teach lessons.

A good teacher changes lives.

Vinegar Water and Real Life

Monique and I were not expecting a lesson that day.

"Go wash and clean out that refrigerator," Mrs. Grace said, pointing toward the kitchen as casually as if she were assigning multiplication tables.

I looked at Monique.

Monique looked at me.

Clean the refrigerator?

We knew how to sweep. We knew how to wash dishes. We even knew how to fold towels into crooked squares. But a refrigerator? That felt official. Important. Grown-up.

Still, we obeyed.

We opened the refrigerator door and stared inside as if it were a cold cave of confusion. There were jars filled with mystery sauces, leftovers wrapped in foil, bottles with crusted tops, and containers pushed so far to the back they seemed to belong to another decade.

"Well... let's just wipe it," Monique whispered.

I nodded with confidence I did not really feel.

We began pulling a few things out and setting them on the counter. We wiped around bottles instead of removing them. We cleaned what we could see and left the rest alone. When we were done, we closed the door proudly.

It looked better.

At least to us.

When Mrs. Grace came to inspect it, she did not say anything at first. She opened the refrigerator slowly. She moved a jar. She lifted a bowl. Then she bent down and looked into the vegetable drawer.

Her face changed.

Not angry.

Not yelling.

Just surprised.

And a little disappointed.

"You mean to tell me," she said gently, "you don't know how to clean a refrigerator?"

I felt heat rise in my cheeks. No one had ever shown me how. I knew about cleaning, but cleaning correctly was something different.

Mrs. Grace did not scold us.

She taught us.

"First," she said, "you remove everything. Everything means everything."

Out came the jars. The bowls. The forgotten leftovers. The sticky bottles.

"Now," she continued, "you check the dates. If it's expired, it goes in the trash. If you don't know what it is, it goes in the trash. If it smells funny, it definitely goes in the trash."

That day I learned that keeping something just because it was there was not a good enough reason.

Mrs. Grace mixed vinegar and water in a bowl.

"No fancy cleaners needed," she said. "Vinegar water will do."

The sharp smell filled the kitchen. It smelled clean. Honest. Real.

She showed us how to remove the shelves completely. I had not even realized they could come out.

"Take it apart," Mrs. Grace instructed. "You can't clean around something. You clean under it. Behind it. Inside it."

We wiped each shelf carefully with vinegar water. We scrubbed the corners. We washed the drawers and dried every surface before putting it back.

Then we reorganized everything. Milk in its place. Vegetables where they belonged. Condiments standing upright instead of leaning like tired soldiers.

When we finished, the refrigerator did not just look clean.

It looked cared for.

Mrs. Grace nodded.

"That," she said, "is how you clean a refrigerator."

I stood a little taller.

School was not just about books anymore.

It was about life.

It was about learning how to look at something closely. How to remove what did not belong. How to throw away what had expired. How to clean with what you had. How to restore order.

Vinegar water and real life.

That day I learned that education does not always happen at a desk.

Sometimes it happens in a kitchen.

Sometimes it smells like vinegar.

And sometimes the greatest lessons are hidden behind a refrigerator door.

8

Mrs. Grace Didn't Sit Down

Mrs. Grace did not teach from a chair.

She walked.

That may not sound important, but to us it was everything.

She moved through the room as if the room belonged to her. She stood at the chalkboard. She leaned over desks. She checked handwriting. She looked at our work while we were doing it, not after we had already made every mistake.

She taught with her whole body.

Her heels clicked through the aisles. Her curls bounced when she turned. Her voice reached the front row and the back row because she did not stay in one place long enough for anyone to feel forgotten.

Even the sixth graders noticed.

Especially the sixth graders.

She went all the way to the back of the room, where other teachers had barely gone. She looked at their papers. She corrected them on the spot. She made them sit up. She made them answer.

No one could hide in Mrs. Grace's classroom.

And strange as it may seem, that felt good.

Being seen can be uncomfortable when you are used to disappearing.

But it can also feel like care.

Mrs. Grace did not sit down because she was teaching more than lessons.

She was teaching attention.
She was teaching accountability.
She was teaching us that leadership moves toward people, not away from them.

That was one of the first things I noticed.
And one of the last things I forgot.

9

The Gold Cadillac

Mrs. Grace did not drive an ordinary car.
She drove a gold Cadillac Coupe DeVille.

Huge.

Shiny.

Nothing like any teacher's car.

It did not whisper when it arrived.

It announced itself.

Every morning, students waited.

Not for the bell.

For the turn.

For the moment that long gold body would glide around the corner.

The sun would hit it just right.

It gleamed.

Chrome sparkling.

Paint glowing.

Windows shining.

Other teachers drove small cars.

Simple cars.

Practical cars.

Mrs. Grace drove presence.

The Cadillac Coupe DeVille was long and confident, with curves that looked like they belonged in a parade. When she stepped out, dressed neatly, walking tall, it felt like royalty arriving.

Students would whisper.

"That's her car."

"That's Mrs. Grace."

We felt proud.

As if her car somehow belonged to all of us.

It became part of her legend.

The gold Cadillac meant excellence.

It meant success.

It meant you could be educated, disciplined, organized, and still shine.

In a world that did not always show us images of power that looked like us, that car mattered.

It told us something without speaking:

You can be brilliant.

You can be polished.

You can stand out.

And you do not have to shrink.

Every morning, when that gold Cadillac pulled up, it reminded us that our classroom was not ordinary.

Neither was our teacher.

And neither were we.

But the morning arrival was only half of it.

The real parade happened in the afternoon.

Every day, when school ended, Mrs. Grace gathered her things. Boxes. Bags. Papers stacked high. Sometimes art supplies. Sometimes record books. Sometimes things for the club.

And without being asked, a small crowd would form.

Four or five students, sometimes more, would walk with her.

Not because we had to.

Because we wanted to.

We followed her down the sidewalk, past the edge of the school-yard, toward the church parking lot down the street where she parked her gold Cadillac.

It felt important.

Like we were part of something official.

She would hand one of us a box. Another carried a bag. Someone else balanced whatever else needed to go. We walked carefully, proudly.

The church parking lot felt like a runway.

And there it was.

Huge.

Shiny.

Waiting.

The gold Cadillac Coupe DeVille.

We loaded the trunk gently.

Closed it with care.

Sometimes we lingered, not quite ready to leave.

Mrs. Grace would thank us.

Her voice firm, but warm.

"See you tomorrow."

And just like that, she would slide into that long gold car, turn the key, and glide away.

We would stand there watching until she turned the corner.

Every day, a parade.

Not for a celebrity.

Not for applause.

But for a teacher who carried herself like excellence.

We were not just walking her to her car.

We were walking beside greatness.

And we knew it, even then.

The Grace Club

Friday afternoons always felt softer than the rest of the week. Lunch was over, and the hum of our classroom settled into a quiet rhythm. That was when Mrs. Grace stood at the front of the room with that look, the one that meant something new was about to happen.

She clapped once.

"We are starting a club."

The whole room lifted.

A club?

I loved the sound of that. A club meant belonging. It meant membership. It meant being part of something special that we all shared.

Mrs. Grace turned to the chalkboard.

"Every club needs a name," she said. "You will vote."

She wrote three names carefully:

Grace Gang

Grace Club

Grace Club One

The chalk tapped softly as she finished writing.

I studied the list as if it were a very serious decision, because to me, it was.

Grace Gang.

I liked the way it sounded. The two Gs made me smile. G.G. It felt strong and balanced, like the letters belonged together. It reminded me of the television show *Our Gang*, the Little Rascals, that we watched sometimes. A group of children having their own adventures, making their own fun, and living in their own little world.

I imagined us like that, our own classroom version of the Little Rascals.

When it was my turn, I raised my hand confidently.

"I vote for Grace Gang."

Other voices chimed in around the room.

"Grace Club!"

"Grace Club One!"

Mrs. Grace made tally marks beside each name.

I watched carefully as the chalk marks grew. One line. Two. Three. I could feel something important happening. This was not pretend. This was a real vote.

My vote counted.

Just like everyone else's.

Finally, Mrs. Grace turned around.

"The winner is... Grace Club."

I blinked.

Grace Club?

Not Grace Gang.

I felt the tiniest sting of disappointment, just a little pinch. My double Gs had lost.

But no one argued.

No one complained.

The vote had spoken.

Grace Club it would be.

And just like that, I learned something I would understand even more clearly years later: sometimes you participate fully and still do not win, but your voice still matters.

That Friday, democracy did not feel like a big textbook word.

It felt simple.

You choose.

You count.

You accept.

And then you move forward together.

Grace Club became ours, not because everyone agreed, but because everyone had a say.

That day I realized that belonging is not about getting your way.

It is about being included in the process.

A club of our own.

Even if it did not have two Gs.

Officers and Elections

Grace Club did not stay simple for long.

Once the name was chosen, Mrs. Grace stood again at the front of the room and made it official.

"If we are going to have a club," she said, "we need officers."

She wrote the titles carefully on the board:

President

Vice President

Secretary

Treasurer

The words felt important to me. Organized. Grown.

She explained each role.

"The President leads meetings."

"The Vice President assists and steps in when needed."

"The Secretary keeps notes."

"The Treasurer keeps track of money."

Money made it feel serious.

Because the club included older students, the sixth graders stepped forward first. Greg volunteered to run for President. He stood confidently, shoulders back, voice steady. Marie announced that she would run for Vice President. She smiled, but spoke with just as much certainty.

Back then, boys often took the lead without question. It was not something anyone talked about. It was simply how things seemed to work. Greg stepping forward as President felt expected, almost automatic.

I noticed.

I noticed how quickly leadership often wore a male face. I noticed how easily it was accepted.

But I also noticed Marie, strong, capable, standing right there beside him.

For Secretary, Lynn volunteered. Her handwriting was neat and precise, and she seemed perfect for keeping records.

Anthony stepped forward to run for Treasurer. He liked numbers and spoke carefully, as if he counted his words before letting them out.

I sat quietly in my seat.

My heart fluttered for just a moment.

I could have run.

I knew I could.

I understood responsibility. I paid attention. I cared deeply about what was happening.

But something inside me whispered, *Not yet.*

It was not fear.

It was not doubt.

It was awareness.

I was still learning how leadership worked. Watching how meetings were conducted. Listening to how voices carried across a room without shouting.

So I chose not to raise my hand.

Not because I could not.

But because I was not ready yet.

The votes were cast, and tally marks lined the board.

Greg became President.

Marie became Vice President.

Anthony became Treasurer.

Lynn became Secretary.

Grace Club now had structure.

I clapped along with everyone else. I felt no jealousy and no disappointment, only curiosity.

I watched how Greg spoke first and how Marie stood beside him. I noticed how Lynn carefully recorded every word and how Anthony counted the numbers twice to make sure they were right.

I was studying.

That day I learned something important.

Leadership is not only about stepping forward.

Sometimes it is about watching closely.

Sometimes it is about preparing quietly.

Sometimes it is about understanding the room before you try to lead it.

There would come a time when I would raise my hand.

A time when I would not wait.

But growth often begins with observation.

And on that day, sitting quietly in my seat, I was growing.

Hot Dogs and Quarters

Grace Club did not ask for money.

We earned it.

Every Friday, we raised funds for our club the best way we knew how:

Hot dogs, twenty-five cents.

Chili dogs, thirty-five cents.

But the very first week, we had a problem.

We had no money.

No starter funds.

No cash box.

No supplies.

That was when Mrs. Grace stepped in.

She did not cancel the plan.

She organized us.

Since we did not have money yet, Mrs. Grace assigned each of us something to bring.

"You will bring the buns."

"You bring the hot dogs."

"You bring mustard."

"You bring relish."

"You bring ketchup."

We all had a part.

No one brought everything.

But together, we brought enough.

And Mrs. Grace, steady and prepared, brought the chili herself in a crockpot.

That crockpot meant we were official.

The next day, we went out in pairs to make announcements to the other classes.

We stood at the front of each room and spoke clearly:

"The Grace Club will be selling hot dogs every Friday.

Hot dogs are twenty-five cents.

Chili dogs are thirty-five cents."

Some students whispered.

Some smiled.

Some started counting their coins right away.

Friday came.

We set up our table carefully.

Buns stacked high.

Hot dogs warming.

Mustard, relish, and ketchup lined up in a neat row.

The crockpot of chili bubbling gently.

We worked like a team.

One person handled the money.

One person prepared the hot dogs.

One person added chili.

Quarters dropped into the box.

Clink.

Clink.

Clink.

By the end of that first Friday, we had sold fifty hot dogs and chili dogs.

Fifty.
We counted the money twice to make sure.
Fifteen dollars.
From nothing.
From teamwork.
From planning.
From everyone bringing their part.
That first fifteen dollars felt glorious.
The next week, we did not have to bring supplies from home.
We used the money we earned.
Grace Club went shopping.
We purchased buns, hot dogs, mustard, relish, and ketchup. Mrs. Grace still brought her crockpot of chili, warm, steady, and dependable.
This time, it felt different.
We were not borrowing.
We were not piecing things together.
We were operating.
Friday came again.
We made our classroom announcements in pairs, just like before. More students came than the week before. The quarters dropped faster.
Clink.
Clink.
Clink.
We wrapped buns.
Added mustard.
Spoonfuls of chili poured generously.
Then it happened.
We ran out of wieners.
We looked down at the empty tray.

More students were still in line.
Our eyes got big.
What were we going to do?
We had buns.
We had chili.
We had customers.
But no hot dogs.
Mrs. Grace did not panic.
She did not scold.
She did not shut it down.
She grabbed her purse.
"I'll be right back."
And just like that, she went to the store to buy more wieners.
The line waited.
Some students held their quarters tightly in their hands.
We stood there, half nervous, half proud.
We had sold more than we expected.
That was not failure.
That was growth.
Mrs. Grace returned with fresh packs of hot dogs, and we got right back to work.
By the end of that Friday, we knew something important:
We were learning business.
Not from a book.
Not from a lecture.
But from hot dogs, quarters, and problem-solving in real time.
The Grace Club was not just raising money.
We were learning how to adjust.

13

Shopping Trip

That lesson stayed with me again on the day Mrs. Grace took us to Smart & Final.

We lined up in pairs, walking carefully down the sidewalk, trying to look responsible enough to be trusted in public. Inside, everything felt enormous. Aisles stretched long and wide. Boxes stacked higher than our heads. Carts squeaked. Cash registers beeped.

Mrs. Grace gathered us near the entrance.

"You will stay in your groups," she said. "You will follow the list. You will compare prices. And you will not play."

She handed each group money.

"Guard it," she said, looking directly at me when she handed me ours. "It belongs to the club."

I slipped the bill into my jacket pocket and felt important.

But somewhere between the canned goods and the checkout line, I reached into my pocket to check the money.

It was not there.

I checked the other pocket.

Nothing.

My heart started pounding.

All I could think was: *This was club money.*

When I told Mrs. Grace, my voice felt smaller than usual.

"I... I lost it."

She did not react immediately. She did not raise her eyebrows. She did not sigh loudly.

She simply looked at me.

"Are you sure?"

I nodded, fighting the urge to cry.

"All right," she said calmly. "We'll adjust."

Adjust?

That was not the reaction I expected.

She shifted items from another group's list. She recalculated in her head. She reorganized who would purchase what.

She did not humiliate me.

She did not announce it to the class.

On the walk back, she said quietly, "When you are responsible for money, you check often. Not just once."

That was it.

Not anger.

Not shame.

Just instruction.

I never lost money again.

Not because I was afraid.

But because I understood.

Mrs. Grace believed in teaching responsibility in real ways.

14

Goldie & Finley

It did not surprise us too much when Mrs. Grace announced one morning, "We are getting class pets."

The room exploded. "What kind?"

"A dog?"

"A turtle?"

"A bird?"

She lifted a clear bag filled with water.

Inside, two tiny flashes of gold darted back and forth.

Goldfish.

Their arrival felt ceremonial.

Two goldfish.

Two new responsibilities.

Two living creatures depending on us.

We voted for their names the same way we voted for everything else, with suggestions, discussion, and counting.

When the tally was complete, we had our winners:

Goldie.

Finlay.

The tank was shaped like a basket, with a bridge tunnel over the top. It looked almost magical. The fish would swim up one side, disappear into the little bridge, and come out the other side as if they had traveled through a secret world.

We took turns cleaning the tank.

Responsibility was not just something Mrs. Grace talked about.

We practiced it.

Then came the day no one forgot.

It was Anthony's turn to help refill the tank. Mrs. Grace showed us how to siphon the water using a straw.

"You start it gently," she explained.

Gently.

Anthony placed the straw into the tank. He leaned down. He sucked.

Too hard.

In one second, fish water shot straight into his mouth.

He jumped back, eyes wide.

The class erupted.

Screams.

Laughter.

Gasps.

Anthony ran to the sink.

We could barely breathe from laughing.

Even Mrs. Grace laughed, that warm, uncontrollable kind of laugh you try to hide but cannot.

But then, just as calmly, she gathered us back together.

"That," she said, "is how a siphon works."

Lesson delivered.

Anthony survived.

Goldie and Finley survived.

And the story survived too.

It became one of those memories we carried into adulthood.

Not just because it was funny.

But because it was ours.

15

The Week I Was Gone

Fifth grade was the first year I had perfect attendance. That mattered to me.

Every morning I arrived on time, lined up with my classmates, and felt ready for whatever Mrs. Grace had planned. Being present seemed important, as if missing school meant missing something bigger than lessons.

But that year, I had to be absent.

I was having my tonsils taken out.

I did not really understand what tonsils were. I only knew the doctor said they needed to come out, and everyone talked about it as though it were normal. Still, the thought of going to the hospital made my stomach twist.

What I didn't understand then was why it had gotten to that point.

I had been sick over and over again, and the doctor kept giving me medicine. My tonsils stayed infected, and eventually they said it was starting to affect my kidneys. The medicine didn't seem to be working.

What nobody knew was that I wasn't taking it.

At school, we had learned about drugs and how people could become addicted. I listened very carefully during those lessons, and I decided I was not going to let that happen to me.

I was ten years old.

In my mind, medicine was still a drug.

My mother trusted me to take it on my own. She showed me how to measure it in the little spoon and told me exactly when to take it each day.

And every time, I followed her directions.

I poured the medicine carefully into the spoon...
and then I poured it into the sink or the toilet.

Whichever one I was closest to.

As far as I can remember, the only dose I actually took was the very first one my mother gave me.

At the time, I thought I was protecting myself.

I didn't understand that I was making myself worse.

The morning of the surgery smelled like antiseptic and fear. Nurses spoke softly. My mother stayed close. I remember bright lights and someone telling me to count backward.

Then everything disappeared.

When I woke up, my throat felt like fire.

Swallowing hurt.

Talking hurt.

Even breathing felt sharp.

Everyone kept offering me ice cream and Popsicles, saying that was the best part about getting your tonsils out. But my throat hurt so badly that I refused to eat. Nothing felt safe to swallow. I lived mostly on Popsicles, ice cream, and Jell-O, and even that hurt going down.

It was also my first time taking the red liquid Tylenol they gave me for pain. I watched carefully as the nurse poured it into a small plastic cup. Even though I was ten years old, I still could not swallow pills, so the medicine came thick and sweet, sliding slowly down my sore throat.

I shared a hospital room with another little girl who had her tonsils removed the same day. By the very next day, she was eating hamburgers and fries as if nothing had happened. I watched in disbelief as trays came and went from her side of the room.

Meanwhile, I was still carefully sipping melted Popsicles.

I remember wondering how she could possibly eat real food while I could barely swallow.

The days moved slowly.

One of the highlights of my recovery was watching an old movie on television starring Lucille Ball called *Yours, Mine and Ours*. She played a mother with eight children who married a military man with ten of his own, and together they added one more child to the family. I loved that movie. The house was loud and busy, full of children everywhere, and somehow it made me feel better to watch a family manage chaos with laughter.

While my throat hurt and I barely spoke, I watched that movie and forgot about the pain for a while.

I missed a whole week of school, my first absence in fifth grade.

In fourth grade, being absent had felt different. Sometimes I stayed home to help my aunt with my baby cousin. Back then, cars did not have seatbelts the way they do now. Car seats were not required, and the infant seats they used were flimsy plastic with a thin wire on the back. If I had not been there to hold him while she drove, she would have had to place him on the floor in that little seat.

So I held him.

Carefully.

Proudly.

It felt like responsibility, not absence.

But this time was different. This time I was not helping anyone. I was just sick and missing everything.

A week later, I returned to the doctor for my follow-up appointment. That was when we discovered something surprising.

I had lost ten pounds.

No wonder my clothes felt loose.

When I finally returned to school, my uniform hung differently on my body. Everyone noticed.

"You look skinny," someone said.

My throat still hurt when I talked, and my voice sounded smaller than before. Walking back into the classroom felt almost like the first day again. The desks were the same. The chalkboard was the same. Mrs. Grace stood at the front like always.

But when she saw me, she smiled in a way that made it clear I had been missed.

"Welcome back," she said simply.

Not dramatic.

Not loud.

Just certain.

I sat down at my desk and picked up my work again, grateful in a way I had never been before.

That week taught me something unexpected.

School was not just a place I went every day.

It was a place where I belonged.

And being gone long enough to feel its absence made returning feel like coming home.

Names in a Bowl

December brought excitement wrapped in mystery.

One morning Mrs. Grace placed a bowl on her desk.

Inside were slips of paper, each with one of our names.

"We will each pull one name," she explained, "and buy a gift for that person."

One gift.

One name.

A secret.

We lined up and reached into the bowl.

Each of us unfolded our paper carefully, trying not to react too loudly when we saw the name.

I pulled Lynn's.

Lynn loved the crocheted vest I wore, the one I was so proud of. She would run her fingers across the stitching and tell me how pretty it was.

So I found her one.

Not the same color, but the same style.

I wrapped it carefully and waited for gift day.

When the day finally arrived, the classroom looked different.

Desks were pushed aside.

There was food.

Music.

Laughter.

We ate.

We danced.

Then we began opening gifts.

One girl gave a boy about twelve pairs of socks.

He tried to smile.

But he was not happy.

We could tell.

In the middle of the celebration, Donnell began asking quietly around the room.

"Did anyone pull my name?"

We looked at each other.

One by one we realized something strange.

None of us had pulled Donnell's name.

He asked again.

"Did anybody get me?"

His voice was softer this time.

The room felt different now.

Heavy.

We started wondering if his name had somehow been left out of the bowl.

Donnell sat there for the rest of the party trying to be brave, trying to act like it did not matter.

But it did.

Then Mrs. Grace called his name.

"Donnell, come here."

He walked slowly to her desk, not sure what was about to happen.

Mrs. Grace smiled.

"I have something for you," she said.

She reached under her desk and pulled out a medium-sized box with a big red bow on top and handed it to him.

A broad smile spread across Donnell's face.

"Thank you! Thank you!" he said excitedly.

He tore the paper off the box and opened it immediately.

Inside was a bright red remote-control car.

He loved it.

Donnell hugged the car first.

Then he carefully set it on the floor and wrapped his arms around Mrs. Grace.

She laughed softly and hugged him back.

"Was it worth the wait?" she asked.

Then she explained, "My son helped me pick it out for you. I chose your name out of the bowl."

Donnell looked down at the car again, still smiling.

"I hope you enjoy your gift," she said.

He did.

And just like that, the heaviness in the room disappeared.

The party started again.

But we all learned something that day.

Good things come to those who wait.

The Recorder Revolution

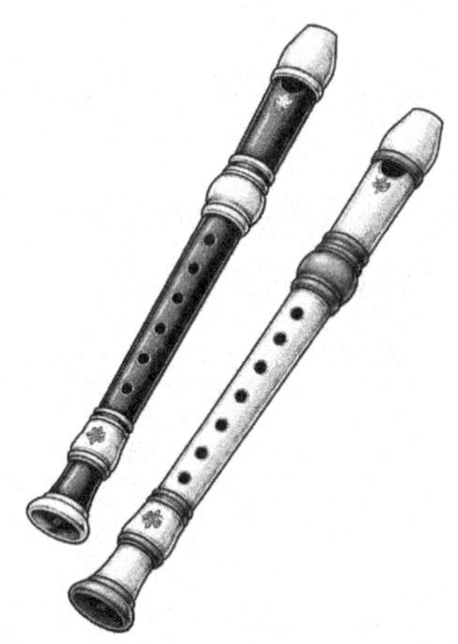

One afternoon, Mrs. Grace opened a long cardboard box and placed it carefully on her desk.

We leaned forward all at once.

Inside were instruments.

Recorders.

Some were white trimmed in red. Others were black trimmed in ivory. They looked serious — not like toys, but like something important. Something official.

Mrs. Grace lifted one gently.

"These," she said, "are Flute-o-phones."

So that is what we called them.

Flute-o-phones.

She passed them out one by one. The boys received the black recorders. The girls received the white ones trimmed in red. Even that felt organized, intentional — like we were part of an orchestra instead of an elementary classroom.

And then it began.

Squeaks.

Wrong notes.

Laughter.

Someone blew too hard. Someone forgot to cover the holes. Someone made noise just because they could.

Mrs. Grace raised her hand.

"Sit up straight."

The room quieted.

"Cover the holes completely."

She demonstrated slowly.

"Blow softly. Music is not forced — it is controlled."

We tried again.

Still squeaks.

Still laughter.

But now there was rhythm inside the chaos.

I had taken piano lessons, so the notes made a little sense to me. Do. Re. Mi. Lines and spaces were not strangers. While others searched for sounds, I began to see patterns.

By February, Mrs. Grace made an announcement.

"For our performance," she said, "we will play *We Shall Overcome*."

The room grew still.

This was no longer practice.

This was preparation.

She paired students together.

"Denise and Anthony."

We looked at each other, surprised.

"You will learn the song," she said, "and then you will help teach it to the class."

Teach it.

Not just play it.

I took my white recorder home every afternoon. I practiced slowly, covering each hole carefully, listening for the melody to appear. Some nights the notes sounded beautiful. Other nights they sounded tired and uneven.

Then something new started happening.

The phone would ring in the evening.

My mother would answer and call my name.

"It's your teacher."

Mrs. Grace.

She called us at home before performances.

"Get your recorder," she would say calmly through the receiver.

I would stand near the telephone cord stretched tight across the room and play while she listened on the other end of the line.

"Again," she would say.

"Slow down."

"Cover the holes."

She could hear everything — every mistake, every rushed breath, every missed note — through that telephone.

She wasn't checking on us.

She was preparing us.

She wanted us ready.

When performance day came, we didn't just play music — we looked like a group. Mrs. Grace believed presentation mattered as much as sound. We dressed in matching colors so we would appear neat and uniform.

One time, we even performed wearing our May Day dresses — long navy blue and white checkered maxi dresses that moved when we walked. The boys stood beside us in dark pants and white shirts, recorders held carefully in their hands.

White instruments.

Black instruments.

Different colors.

One sound.

Standing there together, I realized this was bigger than music. Mrs. Grace wasn't just teaching notes. She was teaching discipline, pride, and preparation.

When we finally played *We Shall Overcome*, the melody moved smoothly from one recorder to the next.

No squeaks.

No laughter.

Just music filling the room.

And in that moment, holding my white recorder trimmed in red, dressed like part of something organized and beautiful, I felt it—

Confidence.

Responsibility.

Belonging.

Mrs. Grace didn't just teach us how to play an instrument.

She taught us how to show up ready.

And when the last note faded, we understood something without anyone saying it aloud:

Excellence is practiced long before the performance begins.

18

Black History Week

Historian Dr. Carter G. Woodson started something called Negro History Week in February 1926. He wanted people to learn about the accomplishments of Black Americans that were often left out of books. He chose the second week of February because it included the birthdays of Abraham Lincoln and Frederick Douglass.

At the time, I didn't know all of that.

All I knew was that when I walked into the classroom that Monday morning, something felt different.

The walls were no longer plain.

Beside every desk hung a large poster of a Black leader. Men and women looked out at us as we took our seats. The room felt fuller, almost quiet in a different way, like something important had entered the space.

I looked at the wall beside my desk.

My person was Mary McLeod Bethune.

Her picture showed a woman with calm, steady eyes. Underneath was a short story about her life. I leaned closer and read every word.

She had started a school with five children.

They didn't have desks.

They didn't even have a building.

They sat on milk crates under a tree.

Milk crates.

Under a tree.

I tried to picture it. The sun shining down. The tree giving just enough shade. Children sitting carefully on wooden crates while she taught them anyway.

That part stayed with me.

She didn't wait for everything to be perfect.

She just started.

The little school grew.

It became Bethune-Cookman University.

A college.

I remember staring at that sentence, trying to understand how something so small could become something so big. I didn't have the words for it then, but I knew it mattered.

There was another part that said she helped start something called the National Council of Negro Women.

I didn't understand that part at all.

The words sounded important, but far away. National. Council. Negro Women. They felt like grown-up words for grown-up people.

I was just a girl sitting at a desk, reading a poster during Black History Week.

All I knew was that she built something.

And somehow, that felt important to me.

Mrs. Grace didn't rush us that week.

She let us read.

She let us ask questions.

She let us sit with what we were learning.

Years later, I would understand what that moment really meant.

I grew up.

And one day, I found myself serving as president of a section of the very organization whose name I once did not understand.

The National Council of Negro Women.

Suddenly, that poster was no longer just paper on a wall.

It was part of a story.

A story that had quietly connected itself to my life long before I knew it.

Black History Week was meant to teach us about people who came before us.

But what I didn't understand as a child was this:

Sometimes history is not just something you study.

Sometimes, it waits for you to grow into it.

19

The Puddle

When it rained, the playground changed.

The dirt packed hard beneath our shoes loosened and darkened, and right in the center of everything, exactly where it would cause the most inconvenience, a large puddle formed. Not near the fence. Not tucked away in a corner. But in the very middle of the yard, stretching wide and stubborn, as if it knew it was in charge.

The problem was where it sat.

The playground equipment was on the other side of that puddle. The jungle gym. The merry-go-round. The sliding board. All the places that mattered were just beyond it, separated from us by a wide, muddy lake we were not supposed to cross. We would stand on one side, staring longingly across the water as if the equipment had moved miles away instead of a few feet.

One recess, after a particularly heavy rain, the puddle was enormous. It swallowed the center of the yard and shimmered as if daring someone to challenge it.

And then someone did.

There was a car tire sitting right in the middle of the puddle. No one knew how it got there. Maybe it had once belonged to old playground equipment. Maybe it had washed loose from somewhere.

But there it was, half submerged, floating just enough to make things interesting.

The fifth and sixth graders saw opportunity.

They lined up and began taking turns jumping over the tire. Not into the puddle. Not through it. Over it. A running start, knees high, clearing the rubber circle as if it were an Olympic event. Each successful jump brought cheers and splashes.

The puddle no longer seemed like a barrier.

It had become a stage.

Then my sister's class came out.

She was in fourth grade. Close enough in age to be brave. Far enough away to still be proving something. They watched the older kids for a moment and then, of course, they tried it too.

One by one, they ran.

One by one, they jumped.

And then it was her turn.

She ran toward the tire, arms pumping, determined to clear it just like the older kids. She jumped, but instead of flying over, she dropped straight down.

Right into the middle of the tire.

She landed sitting perfectly inside the hollow center, water splashing up around her like a crown. For a split second, everything froze.

Her eyes were wide with surprise. Her mouth opened like she was about to say something, but no words came out. Water dripped from her braids, and her dress clung to her legs.

Then everyone laughed.

Not cruel laughter. Not mocking laughter. Just the uncontrollable kind that bubbles up when something unexpected happens. It was the picture of it, her sitting there in the middle of that tire, surprised, soaked, and stunned.

She looked around at all of us laughing and made a face somewhere between embarrassment and disbelief, like she could not quite decide whether to laugh too or start crying.

One of the older students finally stepped forward and reached down.

"Come on," he said, grabbing her hands.

Two of them pulled her up from the tire, and when she stood, water poured out of the rubber ring and splashed back into the puddle. Her shoes squished when she tried to walk.

The laughter slowly faded as we realized she was completely soaked from the waist down.

A teacher hurried across the playground.

"What happened here?" she asked, already knowing the answer.

No one spoke.

We all just stood there looking at the puddle, the tire, and my sister standing in the middle of it with wet socks and muddy shoes.

"Well," the teacher said, trying not to smile, "someone needs to go to the office."

My sister looked down at her clothes and then back at the teacher with a small sigh, the kind children make when they know the adventure is over.

She was gently guided across the playground toward the school building so she could change into dry clothes.

The laughter echoed behind her.

And then it stopped.

Because teachers do not find humor in puddle Olympics.

We all got in trouble.

Not for laughing.

For jumping.

The tire was not school equipment. The puddle was not a game. And the playground, apparently, was not meant to be crossed that way. It did not matter that the older kids started it. It did not matter that the equipment was stranded on the other side.

What mattered was that we were not supposed to be in that water.

Standing there afterward, shoes wet, socks heavy, laughter swallowed, I realized something about childhood rules.

Sometimes the biggest trouble does not come from what makes us laugh.

It comes from trying to cross what has been placed in the middle of our way.

But I also realized something else.

Children are natural risk-takers.

We watch.

We measure.

We imagine we can do what the bigger kids do.

Sometimes we soar.

And sometimes we land sitting in the middle of a tire in a muddy puddle.

Either way, childhood keeps moving forward—learning, trying, falling, getting back up, and running toward the next jump.

May Day

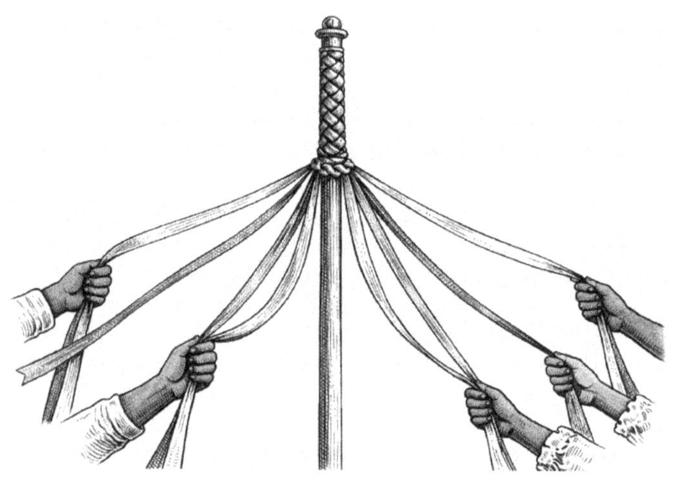

May Day was not just another assembly. It was a full school-wide program: chairs lined in neat rows, parents fanning themselves with folded programs, teachers whispering last-minute instructions, and children buzzing with excitement. It felt like something grand was about to happen, even though we stood right there in our familiar school yard.

Second grade always braided the Maypole.

The pole stood tall in the center, wrapped at the top with long ribbons in bright colors. As the music played, the second graders stepped in and out, over and under, weaving the ribbons in perfect rhythm until a beautiful pattern formed around the pole. It was tradition. It was choreography. It was art made by children's hands.

There was always a Queen's Court.

A king, a queen, four princesses, and four princes.

They were not chosen by grades or votes. They were chosen by who sold the most candy during the candy drive. Candy bars meant crowns. Sales meant sashes. I had been on the Queen's Court once, in second grade. I remember the thrill of hearing my name, the way the crown felt heavier than I expected, and the pride shining on my mother's face. But after that year, my name was never called again. I cheered for others, smiled politely, and clapped as they walked across the stage in satin and sparkle.

This particular year felt different.

Our class was dancing to "Am I Black Enough for You" by Billy Paul. It was the 1970s, and that song carried confidence, identity, and pride. Even as children, we felt the power of it. We did not fully understand all the lyrics, but we understood the feeling. It was bold. It was unapologetic.

The girls wore what they called maxi dresses, long navy blue and white checkered dresses that brushed our ankles when we moved. They swayed when we turned. Parents had to go to the children's store to buy them, and everyone showed up dressed exactly alike. The boys wore black pants, white shirts, and ties. They looked sharp standing tall beside us.

My mother bought a dress for my sister too.

Even if she was not dancing that year, she would not be left out. That was my mother's way. If one of us had something special, the other would too. When we stood side by side in our matching navy and white checks, we looked like we belonged to something bigger than ourselves.

On May Day, the school yard felt like a stage and a sanctuary all at once. The music, the Maypole weaving, the crowns, the dresses, the ties, it was tradition stitched together with community pride.

I was not on the Queen's Court that year.

But when the music started and we moved in unison, navy and white swaying in rhythm to Billy Paul's voice, I felt crowned in a different way.

Not by candy sales.

But by identity and belonging.

By knowing exactly who I was.

21

The New Teacher in Room 2

At the end of the school year, a new teacher came to our school. She had her own classroom.

That alone made her important.

But what made her mysterious was this: she did not have her own students.

Every other teacher had a roster, a line, a group that belonged to them. But this teacher? Students drifted in and out of her room all day long. They would disappear from their classrooms for a while and return holding small treats, stickers, candy, sometimes a pencil with a bright eraser.

Naturally, we noticed.

Her room was near the end of the hallway. The door stayed open just enough for curiosity to peek inside. The bulletin boards were colorful. The tables were smaller. The atmosphere felt different, quieter, but softer too. Students did not go in as a whole class. They went one or two at a time.

We were told she was helping students with reading.

Helping.

That word floated around without explanation. If someone went to her room, we whispered about it. Was it good? Was it bad? Did it mean you were smart? Did it mean you were not?

No one explained.

All we knew was that students went in and came out with treats.

Sometimes they looked relieved. Sometimes proud. Sometimes embarrassed. But they always had something in their hands. That made her room seem less like a place of punishment and more like a place of reward.

I watched carefully.

I wondered what happened in there. Did she read stories out loud? Did she practice spelling words? Did she sit close and point to the words as they sounded them out? I imagined soft voices, patient corrections, and encouragement that did not echo across the whole classroom.

At the time, I did not have the language for what she was doing.

I did not know about Individualized Education Plans.

I did not know about pull-out services.

I did not know about specialized instruction.

I did not know she was a resource specialist.

I just knew she was different.

Years later, when I became one myself, the memory came back to me with clarity. The small groups. The quiet room. The intentional instruction. The treats, those small incentives meant to build confidence, not dependency. She was not just "helping with reading."

She was closing gaps.

She was protecting self-esteem.

She was giving students what they needed in a way that did not shame them.

As a child, I saw mystery.

As an adult, I see strategy.

As a professional, I see compassion wrapped in structure.

That new teacher with no class of her own taught me something long before I understood it: sometimes the most important work in a school happens quietly, behind a door that students walk in and out of, carrying more than just treats when they leave.

22

Sister Mix-Up

There were four of us.

Two sets of sisters.

My sister and I were in third and fifth grade. Monique and Monae were also in fifth and third grade. From a distance, people often paused before calling our names. We looked that much alike.

Monique and I resembled each other the most at first glance. We were both dark-skinned with long hair that fell past our shoulders. Teachers sometimes did a double take when one of us answered. But Monae and I shared something different. We were both a little on the chubby side, round-cheeked and soft in the middle. If someone was not paying close attention, they could easily mix us up.

And someone did.

Miss Ellie was the older woman who watched the children after school. Dismissal was at 3:30 p.m., but the extended day program lasted until 6:30. If your parents were working or running late, you stayed under Miss Ellie's care. She had been there for years. I had known her since second grade. She carried herself like a grandmother to all of us, firm, familiar, and full of opinions.

That year she was about to turn fifty.

Fifty felt ancient to me then.

She talked about her birthday party for weeks. She told me several times that I would be invited. Each time she mentioned it, I felt special. Chosen. Important.

On the day of the party, she sent a list of invited students to the teachers.

When the names were read, mine was not on the list.

I raised my hand immediately.

"I'm supposed to be there," I insisted.

Mrs. Grace looked down at the paper again, then back at me.

"Your name is not here."

I tried to explain. I repeated what Miss Ellie had told me. I felt the heat rise in my face as my voice grew more desperate. But rules were rules. If your name was not on the list, you did not go.

So I did not.

The next day, Miss Ellie asked me why I had not come to her party.

I stared at her, confused. "My name wasn't on the list."

She frowned. "Your sister was there, with another girl."

That is when it clicked.

She had given the invitation to Monae and told her to bring her sister.

Monae did exactly that.

Only I was not her sister.

Monique had gone to the party. She came back bragging about the cake, the games, and the laughter. I listened quietly, picturing a celebration I was supposed to attend. A party I had been promised.

I missed it because of a mix-up.

Because we looked alike.

Because someone assumed.

Because names were not double-checked.

As a child, it felt like a small heartbreak, being forgotten without being forgotten at all. I had been invited in words, but not on paper. And in school, paper always won.

Looking back now, I see something else in that moment. Identity matters. Names matter. Precision matters. Being seen clearly matters.

We may have looked alike.

But we were not the same.

And that day, I learned how easily a person can disappear inside someone else's shadow, especially when adults are not paying close attention.

23

Surprise!

As the year began to close, something felt different.

We were not just finishing assignments.

We were finishing a season.

And none of us wanted it to end without saying thank you.

So we did something we had learned from her.

We called a Grace Club meeting.

One she knew nothing about.

It was held quietly.

Whispers instead of announcements.

Plans instead of lessons.

"We should celebrate her."

"We should surprise her."

"She deserves it."

We all agreed.

But there was a problem.

Mrs. Grace kept the Grace Club money for us. She protected it, counted it, and saved it.

We could not exactly walk up and say, "Can we borrow the club funds to throw you a surprise party?"

That would ruin everything.

So we did what she had taught us to do.

We contributed.
Each of us brought money from home.
Quarters.
Dimes.
Dollar bills folded small.
One of the classroom moms helped us. She took our collection and went to buy the cake.
Not just any cake.
A Baskin-Robbins ice cream cake.
Chocolate cake.
Rainbow sherbet.
Bright colors.
Cold sweetness.
Celebration in a box.
The day came.
Mrs. Grace thought it was a regular afternoon. She was writing on the board when the classroom mom slipped in quietly with the cake.
We waited for the signal.
"Surprise!"
The room erupted.
Mrs. Grace froze.
Then she saw the cake.
Saw us.
Saw what we had done.
Her hand went to her mouth.
And Mrs. Grace cried.
Real tears.
Not dramatic.
Not loud.
Just overwhelmed.

Students cried.

Even the sixth graders got quiet.

No jokes.

No whispers.

Just stillness.

Because in that moment, we understood something we had only felt all year:

She mattered to us.

And we mattered to her.

The gold Cadillac.

The Flute-o-phones.

Goldie and Finley.

Hot dogs and quarters.

All of it had built something bigger than lessons.

It had built love.

That afternoon, we did not just eat chocolate cake and rainbow sherbet.

We honored a woman who had given us discipline, democracy, music, leadership, and pride.

And as we sat there together, wiping tears, holding paper plates, watching her smile through emotion, we knew:

This had been a glorious year.

24

A Glorious Year

When I look back on fifth grade, I do not remember worksheets.

I do not remember test scores.

I remember movement.

Hot dogs and quarters.

Flute-o-phones and squeaks.

Goldie and Finley swimming through a little bridge tunnel.

A gold Cadillac shining in the morning sun.

A bowl of names.

A child who was not forgotten.

I remember Mrs. Grace.

And I remember who I became in her classroom.

That was the year I learned how to speak in front of people.

The year I learned how to count money and manage responsibility.

The year I understood democracy was not just a word. It was something we practiced.

We voted.

We planned.

We solved problems.

That was the year I realized leadership was not loud.

It was steady.

It walked the room.

It called you by name.

It squatted down beside your desk and said, "Let's look at this together."

I grew that year.

I learned how to organize.

How to collaborate.

How to adjust when the wieners ran out.

How to teach a song to others.

How to notice when someone felt left out.

I learned that dignity matters.

That preparation matters.

That excellence is not accidental.

And somewhere in all of it, I began becoming someone.

Not because of textbooks.

Not because of homework assignments.

But because one teacher believed fifth graders could handle real life.

She trusted us with money.

With music.

With responsibility.

With each other.

She did not shrink the world to fit our age.

She expanded us to meet it.

That year planted seeds.

Entrepreneurship.

Leadership.

Advocacy.

Compassion.

Years later, when I stood in my own classroom, when I led meetings, when I organized events, when I walked the room instead of sitting down, I realized something.

I was still carrying that year with me.

Mrs. Grace did not just teach fifth grade.

She shaped futures.

Including mine.

And when I think about that classroom, that gold Cadillac, those fish, those hot dogs, that ice cream cake, I do not just remember childhood.

I remember formation.

That was not just a school year.

It was a foundation.

It was growth.

It was becoming.